Pretty Dark Tales

TAYLOR JONES

© **Copyright 2024 - All rights reserved.**

The content contained within this book may not be reproduced, duplicated or transmitted without direct written permission from the author or the publisher.

Disclaimer:

All characters, names and events in these stories are a creation of the author's imagination. Any resemblance to any actual person living or dead, or any event or locality, is entirely coincidental.

Contents

The Jolly Miller 1

Transylvian Valentine 15

Eat Up Sarah 25

Galliano's Last Rendering 50

4 Days 63

Women Of The Spring 76

Dancing A Dark Dance 80

A Moving Story 92

The Jolly Miller

"Do you want me to go?"

Nick didn't answer. An old memory had suddenly come to him and it hurt. His father sitting cross-legged in the sun, patiently weaving thin wicker strips round the frame of the stand he was crafting. His hair was long and he was wearing a red spotted bandana, similar to the one Nick himself once wore. Nick remembered how desperately he'd wanted to help and how his father had taken his small white school-boy hands in his own massive ones, guiding Nick's fumbling attempts.

He wanted to tell Charlie, but she was stalking round the small sunless room in her muddy boots, picking at things, clearly discomforted.

Somewhere something banged shut inside him.

"Nick!"

She stood over him in front of the old Chesterfield chair where he'd collapsed exhausted. "Why do you look so upset? You hated him."

Nick gathered himself together and stood up. He didn't want her here. He wanted to be on his own after all this time. She came from a different life.

He wandered about the room, past the silent computer where his father had spent so much of his time. His pine desk was bare, the drawer hanging open and empty. The wicker stand still stood in the corner but the shelves were broken and the intricate weaving frayed and jagged.

An ancient rage overwhelmed him and he kicked hard at the stand with his neat black funeral boot, muddy too from the graveside. A dish crashed to the floor, a sudden noise, unexpected it hung in the air of the silent room.

He was ashamed of such a show of feelings. Defensively, he glanced in Charlie's direction. "You go," he said.

A pine cone lay by the broken dish. Ignoring Charlie's hurt expression, he picked up the cone and turned it over and over as if it contained a secret.

"I remember collecting these. The forest was dark. The ground smelt of wet moss. My mother was there then and Jess, our dog. I remember stuffing them into the pockets of my shorts. They kept falling out. Mum was laughing. But he wasn't. He shouted and we had to go home." Nick paused. "Why did he keep them?"

Charlie shrugged, still smarting from his rejection. "How do you know they're the same ones?"

It felt like she'd kicked him. Yet even then part of him wanted her to hold him, to comfort him. But Charlie was making ready, tossing her long red hair before twisting it into a knot.

He slammed the empty desk drawer shut.

As she put on her hat with a great show of decisiveness, she turned and regarded him coldly. "What about the house?"

He'd been avoiding that question. "Who the fucking hell knows! It's ironic, isn't it! Fifteen when he chucked me out!" His voice was as thin and hard as a sheet of steel. "Just a kid with nowhere to go. Now he leaves me this fucking house!"

Charlie's fragile face was drawn in a tight line. She'd left her empathy at the bus shelter where she used to sleep. They'd dragged her into the bushes and raped her repeatedly until she nearly died. She had little empathy for anyone after that.

"Stop feeling so sorry for yourself." Her voice was hard.

"Oh right!" Sometimes, he thought, she had no softness in her. But then she probably thought the same. All the layers of pain down the years for both of them.

But she'd gone and he realised he was shaking. He'd been hoping to find something in the room. But even the plant by the door to the garden stood bent, its long leaf-tongues brown and silent. Then he noticed. There was something catching the light in the dead leaves. His father's glasses, half hidden, poignant where they'd fallen.

The doorbell made him jump. He hesitated. His heart softened a fraction.

Maybe Charlie had come back.

He opened the door to see a small wizened woman standing in the porch holding a bunch of golden chrysanthemums. It took him a few seconds to recognize Mrs. Frimpton from next door.

She had a half smile, on her face, part greeting, part condolence. It faded as she looked him up and down, taking in his long dark hair, muddy boots and the snake tattoo on his left cheek.

"Well! It's been a long time!"

Her voice sounded reproachful as though it was his fault.

"I wanted to pop round to pay my condolences. I would have come to the funeral but I had to look after Jennie's children. You remember Jennie...?"

He did. She'd been in the same year as him at school. He'd never liked her.

He smiled thinly. "How are you, Mrs. Frimpton?"

"Oh you know, not as young as I was. But what have you been up to? " She gestured towards his tattoo.

He'd had enough. Today was merciless. "I wonder what you think, Mrs. Frimpton!"

She looked uncomfortable.

"He was on a roll now. "Do you want me to tell you what it's like on the street? Sometimes having nothing to eat for three days because even the food banks have run out."

"It wasn't all your father's fault! I only came to bring these." She pushed the flowers at him and clicked her tongue.

He felt a flash of remorse as she walked painfully down the front path, her grey coat flapping around her legs in the October wind which caught swirls of red leaves and tossed them around carelessly.

He shut the door. He was hungry. He wondered if Charlie would go straight back to the squat. He wished she was here now. He wished someone was here, even Mrs. Frimpton. He stood in the dark hallway, still holding the flowers. He had a house which he couldn't live in. He had a sort of temporary home in London with Charlie. If he sold the house he would have a lot of money. But what would he do with that?

A house that isn't a home, a home with no lecky, with broken windows and a mattress full of fleas. Nothing made sense anymore.

He thought of his mother then. She'd caught up with him once in Brighton. It wouldn't have happened if she'd still been in the house.

The memories flooded back, things he hadn't thought about for years. He remembered her tears when she found the note.

She was standing with her back against the wall in the kitchen. In her hand she held the creased paper as though it was contaminated.

Nick had been fetching a glass of water. They hadn't long been back from their walk in the woods.

"Why does Dad always get like that?"

His mother didn't answer. Her face was white. She was running one hand up and down the side-seam of her jeans for comfort.

"Mum?"

She saw him then, her small son in his grey shorts, looking up at her. And she loved him with such a fierce love.

"Mum, are you okay?"

They'd been for a walk in the forest. He'd collected pine cones and she'd laughed hysterically because he was greedy, trying to ram too many into his pockets like she'd tried to ram life inside her. Then Doug had shouted.

She sighed and put the note in the back pocket of her jeans. "It's OK, Nick." She bent down and put her arms around him. She smelt of the forest, musky and exciting. He relaxed into her hug. But it wasn't safe.

She was trembling.

His father came into the kitchen, banging the door against the red door-stop as he always did. His mother stood up.

Nick looked up at her face and it wasn't OK. She looked like fire, her eyes huge and terrifying. He was scared. He looked back over his shoulder at his father who was routing around in the blue biscuit tin.

His father must have sensed something because he suddenly turned round. "Cathy? Are you alright?"

Forgotten, Nick jumped out of the way as his mother lunged towards his father. She threw the note at him "You bastard!"

He looked surprised. "What's going on?"

"As if you didn't know. Who is she, this woman who loves you so much."

Nick huddled in the corner of the kitchen. He's never seen his mother like this, like a wild animal. It was terrifying.

His father's face darkened. "You're behaving like a mad woman! What's got into you?"

His mother grabbed the note from the floor where it had fallen and stuck it in his father's face. "This is what's got into me! How important it is to spend time with you. What lovely walks you've had along the river! How much you mean to her! I've known there's something not right between us for a very long time."

"This is ridiculous!" He looked furious. "Francis is not actually a 'her'! Francis is a man I've known for a long time. He's a very good friend if a bit over the top. You're embarrassing yourself, you stupid woman!"

"Am I?" His mother's teeth were clenched. "Well, let's invite her/him to dinner then. "

His father hesitated a second, looking non-plussed. "Great! When he comes back from Australia."

"Oh how very convenient!" Suddenly it seemed like his mother had finally remembered him. She turned and immediately ran to him when she saw him cowering. "We'll talk about this later," she said to her husband.

He shrugged. "Talk about it all you want, Cathy. But at the end of the day, you're being ridiculous."

But you weren't were you, Nick thought now. That was the start of it.

He had to get some food. And drink. Not even an offie here. He'd go to the pub on the corner. Years since he'd been in a pub. What did it matter? They could mind their own sodding business. He was going to get pissed.

The nights were darkening now. The chill wind ripped his khaki coat open wide. The pub was farther than he remembered walking with his Dad. The path was muddy, his black boots slipped, but he trudged on, head down, mindless.

As he drew close he could hear the noise from inside. He paused, his hand against the frosted glass of the door. But hunger drove him inside.

The barman looked up. The expression on his fleshy, bearded face when he saw Nick caused the loud group of middle-aged men at the corner of the bar to turn round. Nick glared back at them and they turned self-consciously back to their pints.

The barman looked familiar. He smiled at Nick as he took his order for beer and cheese sandwiches.

"I'm so sorry," he said.

Nick stared back at him questioningly.

"Well yes, sorry about your father naturally. But also I remember your mother... It must have been so hard for you."

Nick didn't answer. He picked up his pint and his sweaty cheese sandwiches and sat on the brown seat near the fruit machine. The men at the bar very studiously avoided turning to stare at him. Everything he'd tried to forget came back at him now in this place.

There'd been a policeman at the door. There was a police-car on the pavement, lights flashing. It was very dark and his father was still crying somewhere in the house. His mother was in the kitchen, making brownies. It was very bright in the kitchen. Her apron had seemed very red in the bright florescent light. She'd been singing:

"There was a jolly miller once,

Lived on the River Dee.

He laughed and sang from morn til night,

No lark more blithe than he.

And this the burden of his song,

Forever meant to be.
I care for nobody, no not I,
If nobody cares for me."

No-one had wanted to answer the door, so I did. It was like watching a film really. I was one of the main characters in it, but it was like watching myself: I didn't feel in it.

"It's alright, lad." The policeman's breath smelt as he bent over me. "We're here now." I supposed that was to make me feel safe.

There was another policeman on the path. They started whispering something about a 136. What did that mean?

Nick took a long swallow from the can of lager. He was back in the house now. In the room. He thought how strange it was that, in the middle of loss, death brought everything back. Almost as though their lives had been put in a kaleidoscope to be thrown around and churned up. Bright mauve diamonds, orange suns, clear squares churning, green fragments, constantly rising and falling into different patterns, different shapes, different stories.

Maybe he was getting pissed.

Nearly morning now. He could hear the birds waking up, stretching their feathers, beginning to sing. Soft at first, a reedy chirrup, then another and soon a whole loud symphony of bright clear sounds cutting the night away. He went out of the door into the garden. It was damp and new. The crushed grass sank wet and heavy beneath his boots. Somewhere something rustled and rushed to hide underneath the dark bushes. Somewhere distant something wailed.

He rubbed his eyes. He couldn't focus. Too tired. Too much going on.

His Dad hadn't been in hospital that long. Not as long as his Mum. Everyone had said how kind Mrs. Frimpton was. He couldn't remember any of that. Kaleidoscopes, all falling colours.

His Mum didn't come back. They got along for a while, him and Dad. He thought then, for the first time as he walked around the wet grass, the sky getting lighter, shot with pink and gold, that it must have been hard for Dad. He spent so much time on his computer. He'd get angry when they had to go shopping.

Nick stopped to listen. The birds' singing was fading now. They'd done their job.

He'd been so angry. He remembered that. He'd hated his father. He wanted his mother to cook, to cuddle him. He was twelve when he started running away to find her.

"If you do that once more, you're out for good."

His father's face was grey. He'd hardly spoken all the way back from the police-station.

Nick didn't answer. He had such a rage in his stomach. He hated his father. He'd driven her away. He wouldn't listen to his father's friend, Francis.

"Nick, your father's trying really hard, you know. It hasn't been easy for him either."

Francis had patted Nick's shoulder in what was supposed to be a comforting gesture.

Nick slammed out of the house.

He remembered now as he stood exhausted and grey in the early morning chill of the remains of the garden. It had been his fifteenth birthday.

He went back into the house, into his father's study where his father had spent so much time writing. Never time to take Nick to the park, to show him how to drill things, only the once when he'd shown him how to weave the wicker through the stand. Nick looked at the stand now. His chest felt raw inside and bleeding. Had he been wrong about it all? He picked up the glasses from the dead plant by the door. Under the plant a corner of paper was sticking out. Nick lifted the plant and underneath was a photograph of his father and Francis on a beach somewhere. Only they had their arms around each other and there was some writing across the front of the photograph. It read, 'To Doug. With all my love forever, Francis.'

Another shift of the kaleidoscope. Nick laughed out loud in the still air of the morning, cursing himself for his stupidity. Had he really never guessed?

The argument had been terrible. He'd been using drugs by then and wanted to hurt his father. Just pay him back for sending his mother mad. His father had bought him a new music centre for his birthday. Nick had smashed it into bits before the birthday dinner his father had planned. But still his father might not have flipped if he hadn't done a line of coke and then systematically started smashing up the house.

At 8am Nick fell asleep. He was only woken later by the doorbell. This time it was Charlie come back.

She kissed him tenderly. "I'm so very sorry."

He shrugged.

"No! I should have stayed. I'm sure you wanted me to, even though you couldn't say it."

Maybe it would be alright, he thought. Maybe somehow it would work out. Maybe it's never too late and we do get a second chance.

"Let's get some air." Charlie pulled him towards the door. "We can talk. Let me help you decide what to do with the house. You could sell it and we could get somewhere to live. We could be 'normal'! We could get jobs. We could have a family." She started laughing a little hysterically. "Come on, Nick. Let's get outside. It's so oppressive in here."

He took her hand and they went out into the sunshine. He pulled her to him and kissed her long and hard there in the garden. And he might have been happy if he could but just get that song, his mother's song, out of his head:

'There was a jolly miller once Lived on the River Dee...'

The End

Transylvian Valentine

In the shadow of the great mountain where the dense black forest persistently encroaches, a tiny village cowers helpless, a tiny village which the Enlightenment forgot. And every year on the 13th February, as night smooths and spreads her thick shroud over the land, a terrible fear catches at the throats of the villagers and they lock their nubile youths and maidens up, each and every one of them. In hushed voices with faces grim and strained, they fasten the stout green shutters over the casement windows and heave their heaviest furniture against the wooden doors.

Their faith is scant, but they must do something. They must form some barricade against that which is coming, against that which is relentless in its coming every year, on the eve of St. Valentine's Day. So, boarded and barred, locked and spuriously secure, the villagers settle back to wait.

One girl, Gitta, such a pretty blonde girl of seventeen; such fine tendrils of wispy hair curling round her face, a heart-shaped face with eyes as blue as the Tirol sky, yearns for her lover. In the dark cupboard of a bedroom her door is locked.

Her mother and father downstairs whispering together, remembering the year long past when Gitta's own dear sister Shah went wandering off, went far off into the dark forest to return no more. A sob catches deep in Gitta's mother's throat as she remembers the kindness and sweetness of Shah. How she would always care for her little sister. How she would always draw water from the well to help her tired old mother. How pretty she was and blonde, so like Gitta, such beautiful girls. Once there were two: now there was one.

And Gitta upstairs at her little dressing table which her father had cobbled together, writing in her diary, writing and writing. The green-painted oak shutters across her window, not even the moan of the wind outside to keep her company.

Silence, heavy and inert, just the occasional scratch of her pen as she writes to Helmut, her lover. How she writes! The white paper fit to blush at her longings and her great desire for the dark youth Helmut. Tomorrow the sun will rise, she knows it.

Tomorrow she will meet Helmut and he will be her Valentine. He will bring her white chocolates carved like carnations; he will bring her liquorice and edelweiss.

And later, in the moonlight, he will tell her as he always does, that the gifts he brings mean nothing: that the most important gift he has for her is his love, is his sweet young heart.

Helmut, Helmut. Gitta must have him. She must have the dark still touch of him. Tomorrow is too long away. And now she sees by the candle-light, by the quiet strong flame, by the yellow-light, that her dear little carriage-clock has ticked the hollow of the night away. The hour hand has touched mid-night, the very genesis of St. Valentine's Day.

Gently Gitta lays her pen on the heavy lace mat. Swiftly she steals to the casement window to pick at the lock. She remembers her dear sister Shah, but she has not the dark superstition of her mother, but then she is seventeen and in love, what fear can she have? She thinks it's the wolves coming down from the mountains, for what else could it be? Wicked grey wolves, fangs bared, salivating, their gaunt haunches barely containing their flaccid empty bellies, their bellies screaming in hunger: these wolves slinking down from the mountains, through the forest, to the village, to tear the sweet hearts from the breasts of the youths and maidens, always so very cold, always so very hungry, on the eve of St. Valentine's Day. For what other fate could have possibly befallen all those young folk who had gone missing in the past on St. Valentine's Day?

Downstairs in the small scrubbed kitchen a log fire burns in the black grate.

Gitta's mother and father crouch together on the old arm-chairs near the fire. And on the rag mat in front of the fire, their black and white collie, Lech, lies stretched out warming his old bones, like a skinned rug flat on the rag mat. Once in a while he lifts his pointed face and pricks his ears, then, with a sad and heavy sigh settles back into sleep. Every time he moves, every time the log fire crackles and spits, Gitta's mother claws at the sleeve of her husband's frayed blue jumper and he stiffens, listening so hard the silence pierces his ears.

The woman whispers so softly her husband has to bend into her to hear.

"I cannot stand it," she says. "I cannot endure another year of this terror, of this waiting. Gitta must marry Helmut. Tomorrow she must marry him on St. Valentine's Day."

Her husband agrees: perhaps then they will be free.

His wife is staring into the flames and sobbing.

"Such a sweet girl was Shah. I couldn't bear it. I couldn't abide it if - " She breaks off. It is far too painful to contemplate.

Outside the bitter cold weighs heavy on the ground. The leafless trees stand brave and proud against the dim black sky, their branches pricked out by the orb of the moon, bloodless, hopeless, waiting, watching. The weather-cock on the humble spire of the tiny grey church stands out above the forest and in the grave-yard the grave-stones are covered with ferns of frost and icy to the touch. In the silence there is a moan from the thicket where the old stone vault is buried in ivy and ragwort: a moan, very faint, it could be the wind getting up.

But there is no wind.

And that isn't the babble of leaves and bushes blowing about. Growing louder now, a rush of breath, a disturbance of air, here and there, in the moonlight, in amongst the white headstones, crooked and crumbling.

It is coming.

It is coming.

Passed the thick and gnarled trunks where the ivy trails, where it gambols and viciously squeezes, on to the clearing where the road starts to the village, two figures walk, a man and a woman. They are moving fast down the path to the village. The woman is laughing in the cold heavy air, her breath streaming from her wide red mouth, laughing. Her head thrown back, her thick black hair poked out of sight under a ragged black covering.

The man isn't laughing. So dark, so sad, so resigned he walks by her side, a bitter poet, head down, bowed, defeated.

"It would be so easy," he says to the woman, his deep voice hoarse and old. "It would be so easy to find a beautiful young virgin, a sweet lovely girl who would kiss me in my sleep. Who would kiss me and give me my freedom."

The woman laughs harder. Oh how she loves this night!

"You'll be mine," she says, "again and again and again. You will never escape me now. Not when the great pale moon howls tell of the end of the world. Not when the hinge of the world tips and we slide off down the years. Not even then, my love, for we are together immortal!"

With a toss of her hair and a squeeze of his arm, they reach the first cowered houses of the village, the first neat green shutters and barred doors.

"You must go," the woman says to the man. "Go quickly and do what must be done while we still have time."

And in the narrow village street they part, she to the left fork, he to the right.

Hurrying now, passed all the shuttered houses and on to Gitta's house.

Inside the old collie Lech whimpers in his sleep. His ears prick up and he lifts his pointed head and howls his anguish down the years, down the centuries of suffering that this little village has known, nestled here in the dark forest, in the shadow of its fear.

Outside Gitta's window there is an apple-tree, a pretty tree she used to climb and sit upon when she was a child. Is it the tree scratching at her shutters, oh so softly like a little dry twig?

In the dark cold night a voice whispers. "Gitta! Gitta!"

Such an urgent whisper. It sounds like Gitta's friend, Rosa. On the tree outside Gitta's window? This cannot be.

"Gitta, open the window. You must come. Helmut's hurt. You must come. You must come. You must come!"

But Gitta has already fled. She has gone to Helmut, her lover. With her sweet white hand she clawed apart the catch on the window which her father had so lovingly locked. Out the window, down the apple-tree and on to Helmut's house. To call softly in the village street: to rattle Helmut's shutters very gently with a handful of icy stones.

But now the woman is calling from the tree in the dark. She is angry. She sees the shutter is unlocked, is ajar, that Gitta has left it like that so she can climb back.

And oh how angrily the woman rips back the shutters and hurls herself into the room.

She throws back her head in a rage, in a frenzy and, like the grey wolves, she howls to the moon.

Downstairs Gitta's mother and father cling together. They would like to believe it's the wolves come down from the mountain: that it's the fear of the wolves that has folded the old dog Lech into himself as he died right there on the old rag mat in a pool of his fear.

So pretty Gitta looks, her head framed by the dim sparkle of stars. His strong young hands are stroking the pale strands of her hair away from her face, from her mouth, from Gitta's soft mouth that fills Helmut's dreams.

And Gitta's reflection swims deep in Helmut's dark eyes which speak to her, which tell her such lovely wicked things. And Helmut bends his fine strong head, his lips warm on Gitta's. And Gitta yields to him, bends into him, against his broad chest, against the wild hardness of him.

And neither remembers to be watchful.

Neither remembers to beware as they love there, in the cold, in the front of the church-yard, so hot and heavy with their desire.

She sees them there like that, locked together. Through the black trees and the ivy leaves she sees them and she laughs, relieved.

She calls, softly at first: "Gitta, Gitta. Come to me."

In Helmut's strong arms Gitta stiffens. Her pretty heart-shaped face flushes warm in the icy cold. She pushes Helmut from her with a firm but gentle touch and she turns with fine wonder, to the woman.

Then, "No!" Gitta hears herself moan, soft but rising now, like the wind getting up. Rising desolate now through the proud bare trees of the forest. Over and over again she moans. But even as she looks to Helmut to save her, her sweet white hand reaches trembling towards the woman. And even as she sobs low and long, she moves in a wondrous white dream over the icy graves, mindless of the craggy head-stones which scratch her, which graze her as she passes.

Behind Helmut something stirs. The woman looks. The man is there. He is stretching out his hands to Helmut, like a cold white noose to close around Helmut's neck.

"Sweet!" the woman is saying to Gitta. "Come Gitta, my sweet."

And with such care, with such loving reverence, the woman takes her, strokes her long hair so pale in the moonlight.

"My sweet," she says over and over as she kisses Gitta's soft white neck. As she bares her pointed teeth and sinks them hard down into the flesh beneath.

Back in Gitta's house her mother and father still sit, their hands together, listening, waiting. Once they think they hear Shah call out there in the forest. Once they think they hear Gitta answer and they wonder if their daughters have found each other; are once more gambolling together in the forest, in and out of the tree-trunks, laughing together. They cannot hear the sounds from the grave-yard. They cannot hear the last mortal whimpers of their younger daughter and, pray to God, they will never guess at the speed with which her very heart was ripped dripping from her breast.

Through the church-yard, round the head-stones, on to the stone vault whose mouth gapes open, the woman goes. Her hands out-stretched before her bearing her gift which drips scarlet on the cold hard ground.

And yes! By the open vault the man is there, waiting, back turned, head still bowed. And he turns as he hears her. He is smiling. Now his mouth is as red as hers.

And in his hands, still warm, that dripping heart that Helmut would have given to Gitta, torn out of the breast where she had lain her head so many happy days.

And with great solemnity and many strange incantations, the man offers the woman the love-gift of Helmut's heart. And she, red eyes alight, red mouth trembling with a great desire, gives the man her Valentine, poor Gitta's bloody heart.

And, in such a way, in the black forest in the shadow of the great mountain, the vampires pledge their love as the hinge of the night turns and the dawning light of St. Valentine's Day chases them back to their subterranean resting place.

The End

Eat Up Sarah

There was a little girl who had a little curl right in the middle of her forehead.

When she was good she was very very good but when she was bad she was horrid.

Sarah Simpson was a quiet, golden child and often truly wonderful. But as she grew the gold turned to sepia until one day at dusk on her fourteenth birthday Sarah Simpson did something unspeakably horrid.

Now, years later, she sits very still. Her slight rib-cage rises and falls. Every now and then a minute tremor quivers at the corner of her left eye-lid. There are teethmarks in the grainy flesh of her lower arms, amid the brown age blots, amid the moles and downy hair bent low like sea-blown grass.

I was sarah. I am falling now. I am a broken bird, falling soft through wisps of pink and white blossom, into a bed of downy peace.

Long ago Sarah looked like an angel. She still has the photograph of herself propped up on the dull oak mantelpiece. A small child of six or seven with wispy blonde hair, very fine, almost colourless. With big distant eyes staring out of the photograph, blue eyes like an angel's, very pale but opaque, dense like a block of paint in a child's tin box of watercolours, waiting to be used up. Sarah's meaning was directed inwards: she was eleven when she began to mutilate herself.

Be quiet, sarah's talking! No-one listens. I was Fourteen! After I did it they locked me up and fed me drugs. I knew I was bad. I used to bite myself. Before, I used to light my mother's cigarettes and burn my arms. She had a lovely dress, purple shot with pink and gold. With a little white collar. Very shiny material, slipping from my fingers. I wanted to cuddle it. I wanted to burn it. I didn't want her to cry. Sometimes it woke me up. It was my fault. She'd given me her life. I knew I was bad. I was so bad she threw my rag-doll away.

In the photograph Sarah is wearing a white dress and long white socks. She is in the garden of the old house, near the apple tree. The sun is slanting through the bare branches of the tree. It must be a winter sun. Sarah must have been cold, must have been shivering in the photograph, wanting to go inside the old house, to some warmth, to the fire, to the old paraffin heater in the hall. Who took the photograph?

Was it her mother? Was there someone else there? She cannot remember now, this broken bird.

Such a lovely girl when she was young, if you didn't look too hard, if you didn't study her eyes too closely. Why wasn't she a gift? Why hadn't she been given away when she was tiny, when her wrinkled soft fingers curled round anything warm. Someone to love and adore her. Why had she always been a sin?

She used to sit on the end of her bed in the old house, in the tiny room up in the rafters. A pretty bed covered with an old purple bed-spread. Someone had embroidered the tree of life on the bed-spread, intricate embroidery, tiny gold stitches fraying in places where Sarah had attacked them with her sharp new teeth. There Sarah sat, at the bottom of the tree of life, stabbed by the glancing shafts of sunlight, watching herself. She thought that one day she'd catch herself out. She'd look away from the mirror, then turn back very quickly, sneaking up on herself. But she couldn't catch herself. She couldn't get a hard hold on herself.

I loved that mirror. Once it had been in my mother's room, breathing her scent.

But she couldn't look at herself. It was as big as a small coffin. It covered the plaster where the paper had been ripped off. I hated that paper: rocking-horses and rag-dolls.

I was a rag-doll in a room full of rag-dolls. The only one I ever loved was the one I could cuddle, the one she threw away.

The mirror was cracked slightly, the frame gilded and decorated with neat gilt scrolls. A lovely mirror. I'd lie on my bed and watch the reflections in it. I thought it could help me. Then sometimes I thought I'd butt it with my head until the crack got bigger: until my blood ran steaming down to stink warm between my long white toes.

The mirror disappeared of course, along with everything else from the old house. All boarded up and eventually sold. Sarah looked for it once, after she was released. She went back to the small market town, to the junk shops and the antique shops near the squat grey church. She clung to the thought that if she found it everything would be redeemed. The mirror had been hiding something from her. It had a secret. It hadn't told her everything. What was it? What had it been lying about?

She remembered the dark winter nights of her childhood when the snow twinkled hush in the moonlight. She would snuggle down into her cold cotton sheets, under the heavy wool blankets, under the tree of life, burrow down, a thin tiny cuddle searching for some warmth. Such cold blood she had that cramp would grab her like a fearsome thing. Would grab her toes and twist them, distort them: small cold toes plaited beneath Arctic sheets.

I'd open my mouth then and pretend to scream. I'd hope she'd come in the dark to me, like an angel, my mother. But she didn't come. Such pain, mutilating me, twisting me into a gruesome thing. Then I began to think it was right. I'd lie there in the silent buzz and wait for it. I'd move my toes, willing it, tempting it. It was right: I was bad. Then it would come and I would sing with the pain of it. This little piggy went to market. This little piggy stayed at home. This little piggy was being twisted and mutilated because this little piggy was very very bad. I wouldn't move then. I'd lie there and lie there, how exquisite it was. But in the end I'd be broken.

I'd have to move then. Then everything crumbled and flew off in the darkness like dust. Ashes to ashes and I was the dust rising and floating away.

When Sarah was eleven she had a friend to play. Her mother Jean went out to meet a man and for a time she didn't talk about dying. She threw back her head and laughed out loud as she reached for Sarah. Sarah's eyes were wide. This is what she had always wanted. Her mother pulling her gently against her breast and rocking her backwards and forwards. Tears came to Sarah's eyes as she breathed in her mother's scent.

No-one normally was allowed to visit but now Jean said Sarah could have someone in. Sarah chose Elizabeth who lived down the road, a solid girl with a matter-of-fact heart and no dreams of butterflies. They played upstairs in Sarah's room, but Elizabeth was bored. She laughed at Sarah's wall-paper and teased her about the rag-dolls. Then she wandered about the old house, poking in cupboards, peeping in crevices, searching for a secret. She ended up in the bathroom, exploring the top of the old blue cupboard. Sarah was frightened. Elizabeth knocked a lipstick down the back of the cupboard, Sarah's mother's new lipstick, down deep amongst the cobwebs, in the dirt, in the dust. Sarah cried. Elizabeth was cross and embarrassed. She said she was going home and she didn't ever want to play in Sarah's house again and that her mother was prettier than Sarah's and that everyone knew that Sarah's mother was mad and that, in any case, Sarah was a sin. "What's all the fuss about?" she kept saying. "It's only a lipstick." But Sarah knew.

I knew she'd only just bought it. She bought it to wear with her new man.

She bought it to slick over her moist lips, to make them pout, to make him want to kiss her: to make him want to slide wide and deep between them. I knew. It was in a shiny blue case with a gold ring around it. It was called 'Flaming Rose'. I liked that. I liked to think of her as Flaming Rose. I could breathe then. I thought that someday I might be able to walk out in the sun, in the fields of pale barley, with the larks in the sky and the life quickening in the still dark root of me.

It was the only lipstick my mother had ever worn. I hated Elizabeth. I could have killed. Instead I hit her, hard, below her left eye on her birth-mark, ugly thing as big as a dog's dried turd, a shriek of birth.

The cupboard was heavy. It was full of old material and rolls of brocade wall-paper and made of old pine painted a dingy mid-blue. They couldn't heave the cupboard out to get at the lipstick. They needed Sarah's mother's new man to do it, but she wouldn't ask him to do that, to fiddle about in her dust and cobwebs. It was too intimate. And soon after that he left for Leeds and she never saw him again.

I was lying in the dark trying to hear the hushed moon hiding behind the far elm tree. But it was her I heard weeping. She came into my room and shook me.

Her tears were big clear marbles. She said it was my fault because of the lipstick.

She said it was all my fault, she'd given me her life. I felt sorry for her then. Where had she come from, this mad marbled-teared woman who was my mother? She'd never tell me anything. Where was her mother? Where was our family? I felt so sorry for her then. I thought I should do something. It was my fault. I was a sin.

She hit me. She was angry, hurt. I wanted to hurt her. I didn't want her to give me her life. I got dressed in the middle of the night and went out, in the moonlight, passed the far elm tree. I was frightened. I didn't like the dark. There was a dead man in my wardrobe my mother said. She heard me going. She shouted after me. But I was off, up the lane, over the flat dark fields, up passed the haunted house, not too black, not moonless, enough light to see the pot-holes in the dusty track; enough light to dodge the spiky twigs as they hunted out of the shadows after me.

Where the fuck has she gone?

In the meantime thank you for inviting me to tell you my side of things. Jean's that is, Sarah's mother. Sometimes I don't know who I am.

I did try with Sarah. I gave her everything I possibly could. I gave her my life.

What more could she ask? What could she possibly expect in the circumstances?

The past can chase us like a mermaid's tail. I tried to hack it off but it still hung raw and bleeding, trailing behind me like a hacked off gruesome thing.

I think I was happy until my mother died. I think I was fourteen.

She'd been ill for ages. The cancer got her. After there was just me and Dad. He wouldn't stop crying. That made me wild. I never got a look-in when she was alive.

He'd lived for her. She said I was the apple of her eye. To him I was a maggot eating up her attention. He started drinking. I cooked and kept house. We had a lot of cheese on toast.

It was a dark winter's night when he came to me. I saw him first in the mirror. Can the mirror keep a secret?

I don't remember much except it hurt. It wasn't right. Was it my fault? Your father shouldn't touch you like that down there, do other things, down there. I pretended I was a bird flying off out the window. But my wings broke. He cried.

"Oh my God, I'm so sorry Jean," he said. "What have I done? I miss her so much, Jean, so much."

I didn't answer. He started crying again and went. Next day he wouldn't look at me. I washed the muck off the sheets. He never touched me again. Filthy bleeding mermaid's tail dragging in the dirt and stinking shit.

My periods stopped. He noticed my stomach. We moved house to another town, to this house. We didn't take much. But we did take the mirror with its secret.

He told the neighbours I was twenty and that my husband had been killed in a motorbike crash. I don't think they believed him but he set up his dental practice and some brave folk came.

I nearly died having Sarah. He couldn't look at her either and one day he disappeared. Men are pigs.

There was a huge scandal but people were kind for a bit. I didn't want their kindness. I wanted it all to be over. I tried to love her and sometimes I did.

Sometimes I cuddled her to sleep on starry nights, smelling the sweet smell of her fine blonde hair tickling my nose. I read her 'The Selfish Giant' and 'The Hungry Caterpillar'. Her favourite nursery rhyme was the one about the girl with the curl in the middle of her forehead. I could be a mother to her then and love her then when the wind blew westerly. That's my side of it, thank you.

The fucking wind has turned. Where is she? Out in the dark at this time of night. Perhaps something will happen to her.

It wasn't so bad. I scrambled up the coarse grass of the embankment, up to the new by-pass. A dark glistening tarmac ribboning off to London, so exciting it seemed, such escape: all those black cars and the lorries, bearing down, a great thundering inevitability, all whooshing passed, all going somewhere. I sat down on the grass by the stones they put next to the carriage-way to let the water soak off.

And I sat there by the roadside in my striped blue skirt and my short white socks with the fierce grass stubble biting into my legs and the whoosh, whoosh of the cars sliding passed. And I was very hard and cold inside. Where my soul should have been there was a piece of jagged green glass.

Sarah picked up a shiny coppery stone which had a maroon spiral pattern in the centre, like a Roman tile, little maroon and blue chips picked out with copper, picked out of the soak-away stones by the edge of the by-pass by Sarah, thick dust in her nose, settling deep into the pale wisps of her hair. What if some car had stopped?

What would the driver have thought of her – a small pale ghost lost in the night?

What would he have done to her?

No-one stopped. No-one saw her. The copper stone like a Roman tile had one rough and sharp pointed edge and with this edge Sarah began to rub at the back of her hand, hard. Moonlight slanted down on the back of her thin neck, on her hunched little shoulders, the shoulder blades curving out like a sparrow's bald wings, clearly visible through the white cotton of her blouse. Rubbing hard with the stone at the base of her taut little thumb, rubbing down through the first layer of skin, through the dead outer casing until she reached some rawness tinged with blue where little dots of blood began to bubble. A lone crouched figure by the roar of the by-pass, caught in the moonlight, her concentration intense. Such industry! Soon the blood was a trickle: soon it had made the stone sticky. Bad blood. It stuck to her fingers. She put her fingers to her nose and smelt it, warm, sickly.

And I was proud of myself. Such a burn of raw pain in my heart, in my hand.

But it was right because I was bad, because I was a sin. I was taking the dirt out, scraping away the filth. I began to feel clean, to feel wholesome, to feel worthy and a part of the world again. That's how it always was. I thought I could cleanse myself, dispose of myself. Then, I thought, if I could stand the pain, I could go on. I wouldn't inflict myself on anyone else: one day, if

I could stand the pain, I could do something truly stunning with myself.

Sarah loved her rag-doll. She had it for years. It was always there on her bed, lying on the embroidered tree of life. At night Sarah put it on her pillow, in the sweetness of her breath rising and falling, so it would protect her through the night, in her dreams, so it would shield her from the dead man in the wardrobe.

It wasn't a large doll. It was about one foot high and it wore a patterned skirt and waist-coat, very bright patterns made up of patches, reds, yellows, paisley, checks. It had painted on blue eyes and a wide red painted mouth. In places the seams were coming unstitched and the old rag stuffing was peeping out. Sarah kept sewing it up, but the insides were determined to break out.

One day Sarah came home from school and went to her bedroom to do her homework. The rag-doll had gone. Sarah rushed down to her mother fast, her cold glass soul cracking and splintering. Her mother was calm in her purple dress. She was sitting on the stone step by the back door, bathed in the scent of honeysuckle.

She was peacefully shelling peas into a yellow colander.

Very calmly her mother said yes, she had thrown the rag-doll away in the grey dustbin. That it was old and dirty and she wasn't having it in the house. She wouldn't tell Sarah that he had given it to her even though he couldn't look at her.

His one kindness to Sarah: his one gift. It had to go. Like him. By rights, the dress should also go.

Sarah cannot remember what she said. She knew afterwards that she'd been screaming. She ran to the grey dustbin by the gate but the dustmen had been. Nothing left in the dustbin, only some curly brown peelings and a dead snail. With that cracked green glass locked cold in her soul, Sarah stared down at her mother's fair head bent low over the yellow colander as the bright green peas went plop, plop, ripped out of the pod.

Then Sarah knew.

I asked the mirror, how could she do it? Did she hate me that much? That morning I'd made her angry. I'd asked about my father. Had he given me the rag-doll? It always made her angry. She'd never tell me anything. Didn't she realise that I knew that once she'd been fucked? Who fucked her? Bad blood. She had it too.

You don't take a child's favourite toy and throw it in the dustbin, do you? Even if she is very bad. It's a nice world, isn't it, and daffodils blow about.

It was Sarah's fourteenth birthday. She had five birthday cards, one from her mother, one from Elizabeth and the other three from girls in her class. She was surprised they'd bothered. She couldn't make friends. She had nothing to give of herself: it was all going inwards.

Her mother gave her a dress for her birthday. She'd made it on the treadle sewing machine. Sarah hated it. It was purple shot with pink and gold with a small voile collar and a bow in the front. Just like her mother's dress, a present after her own mother died. All day she hated the thought of that dress, through general science and Henry IV Part II, through algebra and needlework. She didn't want to go home because she knew her mother would expect her to wear it. But she was trying to be good.

At three o'clock, in needlework, she felt something sticky between her legs. In the lavatory she was nearly sick. There was blood on her white cotton knickers: that was it, her curse, she was a woman, the bad blood was coming out.

Very carefully she folded a paper towel and put it in her pants, all the time forcing back the tears which would drop like marbles to rattle on the red-tiled floor, so everyone would know. So everyone would know about the bad blood leaking out, down there.

At four fifteen Jean Simpson heard her daughter's key in the lock of the front door. Jean was sitting on the bottom step of the stairs waiting for her, smiling to herself. In her hand she held the purple dress. It was on a hanger, an old-fashioned stout wooden hanger.

I'd made her a special birthday tea, salmon sandwiches and a sponge with fourteen candles. After tea I was going to take her to see the new film at The Regal. I was excited. I did want to be a good mother to her. It's not her fault she's a sin. And she can be delightful. She looked so white and pinched lately. I worried about her. I wanted to put some colour in those pinched cheeks. I wanted to get closer to her. I do love her sometimes, really.

Sarah turned the key, opened the front door and came into the long dark hall. At first she didn't see her mother sitting on the stairs.

The paper towel was rubbing against the tops of my legs. I hadn't cried, but I felt like I'd been in a road traffic accident, like I'd fallen off a mountain. I wanted someone to come to me, to give me some hot sweet tea, to cuddle me.

Then I saw her.

She stood up and smiled at me, that filthy purple dress in her hand.

"Put it on," she said.

I took the dress, undid the zip and took it off the hanger. I was thinking about my rag-doll then: my rag-doll and the bad blood between my legs.

I hit her with the hanger.

She looked quite stunned.

There was a fight, I think. I can't remember much. I felt very strong.

There was a lot of blood on the ceiling.

She looked like a rag-doll lying there, limp and twisted.

I went to the police-station down the road. There was blood all over my arms.

It was running down my legs too, my bad blood.

The policeman with the white hair asked me why I'd done it. I couldn't say, could I. I couldn't say because she'd thrown my rag-doll away in the dustbin, because she'd given me her life and I didn't want it, because my womb was crying marbles of bad blood. Only mad people do things like that. It's a nice world, isn't it, and daffodils blow about.

They thought I was mad. And bad. Both. They talked to me in very low voices. They locked me up and fed me drugs.

Be quiet, sarah's talking! No-one listens. I wanted to take my mirror. They wouldn't let me. They boarded the old house up.

Sarah Simpson was officially pronounced to be a mad bad girl. They locked her up indefinitely in a secure psychiatric unit. From her barred window she could see the neat flower-beds of wall-flowers and daisies. In Spring the daffodils laughed at her.

They kept me there a very long time. My hair went grey and there were brown age-blots on my lower arms. No-one liked me. They were frightened of me.

I used to stand in the corner and bang my head on the magnolia wall. I tried to explain how it made me feel better but they made me eat everything with a spoon.

Later they let me watch television. I watched 'Eastenders' and once I played table-tennis with Carol who had black hair and hanged herself. The fourth time she really did it. No more Carol, just the hole of the night and the brown scream in my head.

Years and years and years. Then one day they let me out.

As part of an economy drive the Local Area Health Authority closed Sarah's unit down. A few of the patients were transferred to Broadmoor and to private institutions. Somehow Sarah was released.

They found me a hostel. They said I'd got some money in trust all those years.

I said I wanted a house. They said, wait a bit, see how it goes.

For two years after her release Sarah Simpson was good. They said she'd recovered: they said the treatment had worked: they said everything would be alright now. They said it confirmed governmental antipathy towards locking mad people away. It was right to put people back into the community, to encourage them to live normal lives, they said. As long as they had the support they needed. And, of course, it made perfect economic sense.

They said Sarah could have her house and on the first Saturday in August Sarah moved in.

It was a lovely little cottage. Upstairs there were two bedrooms and a newly converted bathroom with a dark red modern suite. When Sarah saw the suite she vomited all over it. They said it was only to be expected, that it was the effect of shock, of trauma after being confined all those years. They said it was nothing to worry about.

Downstairs there was a small kitchen, an over-sized hall and a sitting-room with a real fireplace. It was true that Sarah worried about the hall.

The garden was neat and mainly laid to lawn with borders of mixed soft-wood trees. The cottage was at the bottom of a cul-de-sac, quiet and secluded, but not remote. Sarah's neighbours were well within screaming distance.

At last I had my house. They helped me chose it. All that money in trust all those years. How long since I was fourteen? Long enough.

I had my house. In my house I wasn't a broken bird. In my house I could sing and burn myself. It might have been alright, like they said. Except for the dress. In my hall. Draped over the chair-back. No-one else saw it. A purple dress shot with pink and gold with a little white collar. I tried not to think about it. I tried to cut it out of my head. It was still a nice world, wasn't it? And were the daffodils blowing about?

They should have been ashamed of themselves leaving her in that house.

On Monday the dark young milkman with the curly hair came to see if Sarah would like milk delivered. She answered the ring on the doorbell but she wouldn't open the door very wide. The milkman was a persuasive young man with four children, used to having his own way and on and on he went:

"Suppose the weather's bad and you can't get to the shops. Suppose you're ill.

Have you been ill? You look like you need building up, luv. We do cream as well, you know. And potatoes and bread and eggs."

On and on. In a just world he would have got his order.

Who did he think he was! Sex, that's what he looked like. Great bulging bits in his trousers glaring at me. Dirty, a sin, just like me. On and on. Didn't he know he wasn't talking to anyone ordinary? I nearly told him. I nearly told him what I'd done. He wants to watch out. If he comes here again he might have a shock.

Sarah was so angry she didn't know what to do with herself. Up and down the hall she went, backwards and forwards. Then it came to her and she went back into her sitting-room to sit down on the brown arm-chair next to the empty grate. Above her on the mantel-piece was the photograph of herself in the garden of the old house, with the winter sun slanting through the bare branches of the apple-tree.

Sarah lit a cigarette and watched the thin blue curl of smoke wisp its way up to the hair-line crack in the white ceiling.

They'd found me out. The dress is still there in the hall. In my house! She was wearing that dress the day she threw my rag-doll away. It spawned, that dress: it multiplied. She gave it to me. It never went away. I'll catch it out. I know it creeps up the stairs at night. It threw my rag-doll away. It must be purified. With fire. He knows, the milkman. He saw it. He's come back, hasn't he? She wanted to be his Flaming Rose.

I must do something. I know now I'm still bad. One day I want to smell the wall-flowers in Heaven.

Very slowly Sarah held the lighted tip of the cigarette against the white wrinkled skin under the arch of her left foot. It was exquisite, the white-hot edge burning cold, searing her foot, red and black snakes of pain. She held it as long as she could. Then she fell back, satiated, satisfied. Like an orgasm of pain it came to her. But it wasn't enough. She was thinking of Carol who hanged herself and of her own poor murdered mother, all gone, all gobbled up by a world intent on destroying itself.

Once Sarah Simpson had overheard two nurses talking about her.

They had been expressing their concern about her eating herself up. That was it: she decided that was her only logical conclusion. It would be stunning.

I had this brain wave. I was looking at her dress, there in the hall where the milkman had left it and I had this idea about eating myself, disappearing back into myself all tucked away from the world. That it would somehow help the world. I wanted to do that. I worried a lot about rainbows. I thought, if I did that, it would somehow purify me. That it would make me good. To see how much pain I could stand. Like a baptism of fire. There was nothing else for it: it was logical.

That Tuesday morning Sarah took a long time preparing the vegetables for the stew. With great care she diced the carrots, chopped up the Spanish onions, added some garlic, a fresh chilli and some frozen peas. Then she sautéed the vegetables very gently in a large black saucepan on the left-hand front burner of her new gas cooker. She was singing to herself.

I kept wanting to laugh. I kept thinking, it's such a shame i won't be able to sauté the meat!

I got everything ready on the little white table. It was the first time and I wasn't sure how I'd manage it. I had bought some Ever-Ready razor-blades from the shop down the road. In a packet, six of them. I should have used the knife.

I didn't manage much. Little shavings with the razor-blade. I was a bit disappointed with myself. Even so there was a lot of blood and a bright red pool under the little white table. It stank. I think I fainted.

People taste like pigs. There are no daffodils.

Sarah had a purpose now. She didn't care about anything else: she could have been an artist, so driven she was. She thought she could smell the wall-flowers in Heaven. She thought if she hurt herself enough that she could knock on the great brass door knocker of Heaven and God would let her in.

The fourth time she excelled herself. Once again she had prepared the stew in advance adding some swede and some parsnips this time for variety. She abandoned the razor-blades and sharpened her carving knife on the stone step down into her back garden. The knife made a lovely sound she thought, scraping on the stone, backwards and forwards, its large deep blade glancing the shafts of sunlight.

Sarah had bought some brandy in readiness. And she sat now, sipping at it, wrinkling her nose at the pungent smell, sipping until it bubbled out of the corners of her mouth like golden spittle. And she picked up the knife, wondering at the clean blue glint of it, at the teasing frolic of the light spinning off, tempting her. And with a low howl she plunged it into the grainy flesh of her thighs, over and over, how she hated herself.

And somehow or other she managed to cut off a sizeable chunk of herself, before she tried to bite her arms to pieces: before she cut her wrists.

Inside I am pure now. Inside I am clean. I am the clean white picked bones of a broken bird. I am rising now from the wisps of pink and white apple-blossom, from the curve of the world. See me rise and swoop. I am flying off to smell the wallflowers in Heaven. I am fragrant. I am clean.

Let her rise from the earth this broken bird.

Sarah Simpson believes she is entering Heaven.

Shall we let her in?

The End

Galliano's Last Rendering

It all began on a warm mid-summer's day when Tony the builder started work on the Galliano house. He was in his late twenties, thick black hair and a tanned six-pack. Recommended by the family, with eyes the colour of bees-waxed mahogany: heavy dark lashes, lazy sleepy eyes. Francesca Galliano was unnerved.

He was bashing away at her house high in the Sussex Downs, chip, chip, chip at the old cracked rendering on the mock Corinthian pillars. So brown, so physical with his lazy come-to-bed mahogany eyes.

Francesca had forgotten the physical things. She was forty-two and they'd long ago ceased to exist for her. He'd done that, her husband, with his bitter cruelty and his women, always his women. Francesca hadn't known he'd had a wife before her until the family told her, emphasizing the point that she was never to speak of it: never to mention the wife who'd disappeared.

She always knew when he'd started a new affair. He'd come back puffed out in his dark suit, standing pert and high in his soft Italian leather shoes. He'd notice the sky then, the clouds and the scent of roses. He'd touch the white lilac flowers softly, his fingertips lingering as though they were a part of her, his new woman. Francesca never commented but later she'd sit and stare at him over the rim of her wine glass. Once, fifteen years ago, she'd have done anything for her husband and she did. Now it was him she wanted dead. He was ugly, ugly, ugly. Even his face which his women thought handsome still in its arrogant sensuality, repulsed her, for he'd used her: she was an accessory, now obsolete. But this time there'd be no contract: this time she couldn't involve the family.

The builder wasn't ugly, the builder Tony. She repeated his name in her mind softly, over and over. She could have taken him to sit on a high rock in Sicily with the white capped waves pounding behind him and the dense blue sky above his head. She would have painted him then in oils, with deft strong strokes, sure, long and fast.

There he stood now in his jeans, bare six-pack, by one of the white Corinthian pillars which pretended to hold up a corner of Francesca's huge house. And he was chipping away at it. Big hands, tanned, the fingers long and tapering, not a builder's hands, but strong and purposeful, sensitive hands, chipping away hard, mixing the rendering, covering up the cracks. He was singing softly as he worked. His pink smooth lips moving gently; the tip of his tongue moistening the swell of his bottom lip as she watched from the arch of the doorway. And he knew she watched, a paid watcher himself.

Very slowly he turned right round to face her, to stare at her, his thick eye-lashes feeling like a physical presence upon her, sweeping her flesh. She smiled then very boldly, suddenly sure and strong in herself, into his eyes, touching a deep knowledge of him.

It was then that she really decided. She went back into the house, across the parquet floor, passed the huge white vase of dried flowers, to lean against the wall in the cool shade of the dining-room. Her heat for Tony drove her mind onwards, feverishly planning what she would do.

Briefly she remembered those years long past when Galliano had plucked her like a hot dusky orchid from her home high in the hills of Sicily and brought her to England as his wife. She had known nothing of him before except that he was a very distant cousin and that she instantly loved him. The chemistry between them in those early days was dynamite. She worshipped his dark beauty, his swarthy skin, the way his thick hair curled over the collar of his expensive white shirts: his earthiness, his hot caressing tongue, the scent of an animal on heat.

But Guilio, her old boyfriend, was jealous. He'd threatened to tell Galliano she wasn't pure; that he'd had her in the moonlight, in the vineyards, in the dust, with the great heavy bunches of purple grapes swaying above as they cried out. She couldn't allow it. She'd gone to her father, a powerful man in his own right. All part of the same family, her father, Galliano and the elders which meant some blood ties. But the real tie which bound them together was the cartel, the tie until death do them part.

Her father had seen to Guilio and how sad everyone felt for him. Poor Guilio, it was said. Had too much wine one night and stumbled over the edge of Raven's Cliff to bump and bang and tumble against the jagged rocks until his neck broke and his arm was ripped off. Francesca shed a very small tear but she was safe then. Galliano never found out.

Suddenly the loud chimes of the front-door bell brought her back into the present. They echoed through the silent house as she went to open the heavy wooden door. It was Tony, towering in the doorway, blocking out the sun, one hand leaning casually on the door frame. She could have had him there and then. She could smell his fresh sweat, intoxicating.

"I've got something to show you," he said.

She followed him round the corner of her white house, passed the trailing honeysuckle and on up the grass path by the edge of the drive and round to the back of the house. He was walking fast, slightly swaying his lean buttocks in the frayed denim shorts, a mobile phone straining in his back pocket; his legs strong and tanned. She felt he sensed that she was imagining those legs wound tightly around her. She almost reached her hand out to touch him, so strong was the pull, irresistible, magnetic.

He stopped abruptly. "I was checking the rendering here."

She drew level with him, a strong attractive woman, wavy black hair framing a well sculptured face, her slim but voluptuous body taut in the blue dress. Her feet were bare in some jewelled sandals, the straps caressing her ankles. Her toe-nails scarlet, her skin golden, slumbering.

Tony was about to speak, then changed his mind. He hadn't expected her to be like this: it made things more difficult.

They both stood for a moment, poised, silent, waiting. Like the eye of the storm, something would happen, but not now. Now Tony stepped back and Francesca collected herself.

He pointed down. "All the rendering's gone and the bricks are crumbling. It hasn't been done very well. It isn't a professional's work. Did your husband do it?"

Francesca bent down to look. It was near the kitchen door but at ground level. Tony squatted down next to her, next to a clump of white lilacs which grew near the house. Trees carelessly planted, too close for comfort, their roots straining and searching for something under the foundations, trying to undermine the house.

He ran his fingers slowly over the wall. "There was an entrance here. It's been blocked up. Is there a cellar?"

"There's a door in the hall," Francesca said. "And some stairs going down, but they don't lead anywhere. Just to a brick wall."

Tony frowned. He wished he'd kept quiet. Too late now.

The smell of his fresh sweat was dousing Francesca like perfume. A warm gingery pungency that almost made her swoon.

She touched the roughness of the wall, her fingers inches from his. The wall felt alive, the tips of her fingers fired with such sensitivity, as though they glowed and sparked with life. Idly she wondered about the bricked-up entrance. What a wonderful place to hide a secret. But the thought was gone because Tony shifted an inch or so closer.

"Are you alright?" His voice was low. The lilac leaves brushed his dark hair as he leant towards her. Very close to her. Too close.

"Bit giddy," she said. "Too hot."

"Come. I'll help you." His strong hands burnt her shoulders as he helped her up. For a moment she thought he would kiss her. Neither of them heard the footsteps, the expensive Italian shoes on the gravel until they were almost upon them.

"Francesca!"

It was him of course, her husband. Big, dark suited, stinking of deals and tobacco, planted at the corner of her house, away from the lilacs, blocking out the sun.

Tony backed abruptly. "Buon Giorno, Padrone," he said. "I was showing your wife something odd. I think there was an opening here once."

"Get away!" Her husband was angry.

"What's the matter?" Francesca asked. "Why so cross?"

Galliano ignored her. He seemed to consider a moment then turned to Tony. There was something in the look he gave Tony as if something passed between them. "There was a chute to the cellar. I blocked it off. Both sides."

"So," Francesca said slowly. "A perfect hiding place."

Tony frowned. He knew what was coming. "Shall I knock it through and re-build it?"

Galliano nodded. "Knock the bricks out and leave it open to air overnight."

Yes, thought Francesca. Yes.

"I came back for some papers." Galliano turned, impatient to be off. "I'll be late home tonight."

Francesca didn't answer.

He went then. He didn't say goodbye or look back as he strode off down the drive to disappear behind the tinted windows of his grey Mercedes.

Francesca turned to Tony. "I'll leave you to your work. You've a lot to do. And there'll be more when my husband goes away." She smiled at Tony, glancing up at him under her lashes as she moved off towards the front of the house.

Tony was frowning to himself as a nasty suspicion began to take form in his mind. He waited until she'd disappeared round the corner of the house and then he pulled his mobile out of his pocket. Maybe they were right, he thought.

After his call, Tony fetched his sledge hammer and took to work knocking out the bricks to the entrance to the old cellar.

He noticed some odd marks gauged deep in the rendering at the edge of the opening. They looked like claw marks or fingermarks where someone had dragged their fingers or nails with such force in the rendering before it had chance to take and harden. As though they were trying to hang on, to stop themselves from falling.

Tony fetched the cement mix he'd made up for the pillar at the front and very carefully spread it over the finger or claw marks, hiding them and smoothing the cement out very carefully to dry.

Inside Francesca was lying in her oval Jacuzzi bath. She wanted to be really clean. She lay there for hours, topping the water up with hot as it cooled. No-one else was in the house. The woman who 'did' for her had a sick child at home and had taken two days off already. Tony had finished for the day and gone home. She'd heard him revving his motorbike before he roared off up the drive.

It was perfect, perfect. For hours she lay there relaxed and at peace. So many times before she'd lain there working out intricate and always very painful ways of doing it. But they were delicious fantasies which kept her sane or thereabouts over the years. Now she had it. Now she could make it real.

There was a small hand gun in Galliano's dressing-room. She'd seen it once when she was gathering a favourite shirt of his to hide. Quite often she did this just to give him some irritation, to make him cross. In her fantasies she'd never been able to work out what she might do with his body. Now she knew! It was so exciting she could barely contain herself. There was such joy and power in thinking she could actually do it: she could actually destroy him, nullify him, as he'd destroyed and nullified parts of her, her heart, her soul, her hope and her joy. Little had she left of the woman she once had been.

She dressed with great care and downstairs she opened a bottle of Galliano's favourite vintage. She sat at the top of the long oak dining table, her glass of wine before her and next to it, within easy reach, the small black gun.

He always came in the front door. He'd see the light on in the dining-room and he'd come to speak to her. Then she would blast him to hell.

He was very late coming home. In the early hours of the morning Francesca was dozing at the table. She didn't hear the creak of the French door as it opened behind her.

Next day was unseasonably chilly on the Sussex Downs. A sea mist blew in from the Channel and hung over the coastal town of Eastbourne, reaching as far to the west to the city of Brighton and Hove where Galliano did a lot of his business.

Tony was late arriving at the Galliano house that day. He wasn't looking forward to his task. He could understand how Galliano felt, certainly. He'd never himself wanted to be trapped with a woman for life.

There was no Mercedes to be seen, not that he'd expected Galliano to be there. Best to keep away until afterwards. It all looked very silent as Tony skidded his bike around on the gravel at the front of the house.

He turned off the engine and swung his hard muscular leg over the saddle. He stared up at the bedroom windows, wondering. The blinds were still drawn all over the house. Was Francesca still curled up asleep, warm and inviting? Was she waiting for him? He could enter the house soundlessly and search for her. Despite the risks involved part of him still determined to have her, just the once. He flexed his tired shoulder muscles. His body wasn't used to it. It was a long time since he'd worked as a builder.

Round to the back of the house and still no sign of anyone. He checked the entrance to the cellar and wasn't overly surprised. A suspicion had been mounting in his mind. Maybe Galliano couldn't wait for him to do as he'd been instructed. At the entrance to the cellar chute where he'd smoothed over the old rendering, it was all churned up. A dreadful mess. And a stain on the cement, a rusty stain which had spread.

Tony hesitated. He peered in but it was too dark to see anything and he wasn't about to go in. Best not know. He knew about the disappearance of Galliano's first wife. They'd told him how the family had covered it up as Galliano had been the favourite son then. Tony wanted to block the cellar up again quickly. He didn't want to imagine who might be lying down there in the dark and how she might look. He would have liked some time with her but only at her most alive and vital.

Slowly Tony went back to the front of the house. He took off his biking leathers and opened the white paint tin. Best get on before the day went off and before Galliano came back. He wasn't sure whether he was supposed to block up the cellar again now. But he thought he'd better wait. No knowing what other plans Galliano might have made.

At 5.10pm he heard the Mercedes turn into the drive and purr smooth and silky along it up to the house. Tony turned to the car but he couldn't see through the tinted windows to who was inside. He hoped Galliano would be pleased with his work. It might make things easier. He'd be glad when this job was done and he could move on. There was something unnerving about Galliano. Well, for that matter there was something unnerving too about Francesca but the strong hints of her sensuality mitigated against the warning signs.

The car stopped: the car door opened. A soft Italian shoe peeped out followed by a smooth bare leg. Tony gasped, then quickly recovered himself. The stain on the cement near the entrance to the old cellar must have been from something else, maybe an animal or a bird smashing into it.

It was certainly a shame Francesca Galliano looked so wonderful as she extricated herself elegantly from the car. She was dressed in a dark suit with a huge white hat and a black veil tossed away from the rim. Very fine and very splendid as though she had returned from an important business meeting, as indeed she had.

She smiled at Tony as she walked slowly passed him. As she passed she reached out her hand and touched his cheek very lightly. She smiled again, an inviting victorious smile. He had to have her. There wasn't much time.

"You've worked hard," she said. "I'll be glad when the cellar can be blocked up. Mr. Galliano can't rest until these things are done. And I want him to rest in peace."

Tony stared at her. Was she teasing him? Had she done something to Galliano? He didn't smile back at her.

But still he couldn't resist her and he reached for her and pulled her towards him, kissing her roughly. And he was thinking that there wasn't much in his life that he regretted, but that he'd regret this, the death of Galliano's wife.

No-one had told Tony that Galliano had fallen from grace. That they'd come for him late last night through the French door as Francesca waited. After her shock she had begged them to let her deal with it. They were impressed and stayed to help out if she needed it. She didn't.

She led Tony through the house and up the stairs to her bedroom. Despite the risk she had to have him, just the once.

She lifted his tee-shirt feeling his skin warm beneath her fingertips. She bent her head and very slowly licked his skin just above the waist band of his jeans. Tony moaned.

He pulled her up against him hard, his hand searching for the hem of her dark skirt. He pulled it up and slipped his hand between her legs. He gasped. She had nothing on beneath the skirt. He could feel her wetness. He took her then leaning against the door, lifting her onto him.

They couldn't get enough of each other. Like wild animals coupling they could have devoured each other. Again and again.

And much later in the day amid the tangled sheets Tony raised himself from her and looked sadly down into her eyes as he tightened his hands around her throat. But she was ready for him. Quick as a flash she pulled the gun out from under the pillow and shot him in the head. The shock in Tony's eyes was terrible as they darkened and he fell from her with a huge crash onto the floor.

Francesca got out of bed and stretched leisurely. She made a call and then ran a hot bath. They would clear up the mess. They would do what she said. Now Francesca Galliano was The Family.

All was turning out well.

The End

4 Days

Wicket wriggled out of the damp tent nearly squashing Dog. The grass was frosty. It was getting colder.

It was almost lunchtime on Christmas Day but Wicket had nothing left to eat. He'd given the remains of a tin of savaloys to Dog who had just woken up. He was barking excitedly and leapt out of the tent to rush up and down the steep cliff path. Wicket was hungry but not desperate. He'd survived war; he could survive a bit of gut knawing emptiness. Anyway the Day Centre was open in the morning for a free cooked breakfast – bacon, eggs, sausages, mushrooms, beans, tomatoes, bread, all free. Wicket licked his thin split lips. Once he'd been a handsome man.

He stood up and stretched in the cold dank air. His back hurt. His hip hurt where he'd been given a good kicking a few weeks ago. The size of the tent didn't help either but he was grateful for it. He happened to be at the Day Centre just at the right moment when a large donation came in and he grabbed the tent quickly. Wicket could never sleep in a house again, not since Afghanistan.

Dog was still barking manically and leaping up Wicket's dirty jeans. Wicket's eyes were remote. He'd gone back there as he frequently did. Back to the dusty street where the boys were playing football when the plane came. Wicket started shaking as he remembered the terrible roar and blast of the bomb going off. The world stopped for an instant as the dust plumed up. The black and white football rolled out of the dust towards him but the boys were gone. Physically unharmed but mentally fracturing and fragmenting as he wiped the bits of boys from out of his green eyes, his mind fucked.

He shook his head violently. Get on, get on with the day.

"Come on sunshine," he said to Dog who was a little black boy with half an ear missing. Wicket had found him whimpering by the M23 when he was hitching to Brighton. Some bastard has dumped him. Wicket would swing for that someone if he could get his hands on them. Bastard!

Wicket had erected his tent behind the restaurant near the top of the cliff. It was sheltered from the south westerlies and remote enough from the town to feel more or less safe. Wicket hated the town. Always someone after him. If it wasn't the police it was some angry prick wanting to purge the streets of homeless people. Bastards! Fuck them all. Wicket would prefer a good kicking to the police in a way because he couldn't bear the thought of being locked up.

The restaurant bins were a good source of food for Wicket. He'd often find lasagne and sausages which he'd pull out and share with Dog. There was nothing there today though as the restaurant hadn't opened the night before. Strange, Wicket thought, as it was Christmas Eve and should have been a busy night. He was on waving terms with the owner who sometimes brought him a cup of coffee. Wicket would accept it politely and say thank you but the moment the owner had disappeared round the red building, Wicket would chuck it on the grass. He might be homeless and living in poverty but he couldn't bear crap coffee.

It was such a grey old Christmas Day. As Wicket and Dog turned round the corner of the long building the extent of the mist became apparent. Wicket looked out to sea but the horizon was hidden. Sea, sky all merged into pewter. The wind was getting up. Wicket pulled up his collar. Fucking Christmas!

Suddenly a short way away Wicket caught a movement in his peripheral vision. He screwed his eyes up. There was a tall woman climbing the other cliff path from the west. She looked familiar. Wicket caught his breath. He knew her. It was Fly, the mouthy bitch from the Day Centre. Wicket's shrivelled heart skipped a beat. He found her beautiful. He tried to offer her a sleeping bag one time but she blew him out. Wicket's shrivelled heart saddened. He would have liked to love her. He had been trying to be kind to her. When she blew him out he felt his heart had broken into a kaleidoscope of shards spinning round. He'd just wanted a tender touch.

What the fuck was she doing here?

She was wearing a long black coat open to the wind. She was wearing a woollen hat and a multi-coloured scarf. She was wearing a purple pair of DM's. She'd stopped right on the edge of the cliff.

Wicket's hands were shaking with rage. This was his place!

Yet something about the way she was standing. Wicket knew an emergency when he saw one and he dragged the fragments of his mind together to some semblance of normality so he could shout to the woman:

"Hey! What's up?"

Fly turned round briefly like a grey bird silhouetted against the sky before the mist swirled around her.

A dreadful fear came over Wicket. He started running towards Fly. She was looking down now at the waves crashing far beneath against the jagged rocks. The white spray rose in sheets as the waves retreated only to violently smash themselves again and again against the rocks. Fascinated Fly was.

Her boot slipped. The cliff crumbled.

Wicket grabbed her and pulled her back. They fell over backwards onto the grass. Dog thought it's a grand game and barked excitedly.

Fly was crying. She pushed Wicket off.

"Why did you stop me?"

She wasn't angry. Wicket was frightened of her anger. He'd seen it at the Day Centre. Her blue eyes were blank with despair. The tears welled up and streamed down her cheeks, a sea of tears fit to flood the land.

She couldn't stop sobbing. It touched Wicket's shrivelled heart. He put his arm around her shoulders and pulled her to him. This time she didn't fight. This time she looked up at him and there was a hint of gratitude in her eyes.

They stayed there a long time, Wicket stroking her tangled blonde hair. He kept murmuring to her, just soothing sounds, none of them making much sense.

Eventually as darkness descended Fly began to talk. It all came out like a litany.

"I've been homeless five years. I can't cope anymore. There's nothing for me. I have no future. My family disowned me. They chucked me out when I told them what my step-father had done. No-one believed me. I've been in rehab twice. I've been working the streets. There's so much I could have done. It's all gone. It's all wasted."

Wicket with the utmost gentleness and tenderness kissed the tip of her nose.

She stopped crying and stared at him. And she saw then the handsome man he used to be before life in the army got him.

Her hands were dirty but he didn't care. All he cared about was how it felt to have her stroke his cheek, to feel her soft full lips.

It was very dark now. They stood up. Wicket said, "Tent. Down there."

She had a phone and by the faint light they were able to climb slowly down to the tent. Dog was already asleep in it sheltering from the cold. The temperature was still falling. Wicket could feel it in his bones.

There wasn't much room in the tent but Wicket zipped the front flap up. Dog lifted his head and looked affronted at Fly.

Wicket scratched Dog's head. "It's OK. She's a friend."

Dog yawned, reassured and settled back to sleep as Wicket kissed Fly's lips.

They managed to take off most of their clothes and together they lay into that Christmas night loving each other with great tenderness. Wicket thought his heart would burst. It wasn't shrivelled anymore and Fly had found something that might be worth living for.

Wicket remembered how he used to feel before his mind was fucked. He took Fly's hands in his and said, "We'll stay together now. I'll look after you."

And Fly smiled such a warm loving smile.

The next day, Boxing Day, they went down to the Day Centre in the town for their free breakfast. They tied Dog up on the railings outside as he wasn't allowed in. Wicket grabbed a blanket that someone had dropped for Dog to lie on and he covered him up with a corner of it.

There were a lot of people there and Fly felt quite shy as they went in hand in hand. It caused a bit of attention but most of the people there were more intent on food and warmth than anything else. That is until Jack came in.

He was a big man with a shaved head and tattoos all over his face. On his forehead some horns were tattooed.

Fly saw him and squeezed Wicket's hand. "What?" he said and followed her gaze to Jack. He knew him slightly but Jack had been barred from the Day Centre for months for fighting so Wicket could hardly remember him.

Fly was shaking as Jack made over towards them. His face was angry. He grabbed Fly's arm.

"What the fuck's going on here? This is my woman. She works for me!"

Fly tried to pull her arm away. Wicket could feel a deep rage growing in the pit of his belly.

"Get your hands off her!" he said through clenched teeth.

Suddenly like magic they were surrounded by Day Centre workers who had a sixth sense when something was about to kick off.

One of them, Simon, said, "Come on guys. Let's not have any trouble on Boxing Day. Look," he gestured to the kitchen counter where the free breakfast was being served. "Have some food, guys, it's not worth it."

Jack glared at Simon but reluctantly let go of Fly's arm. As he passed Wicket he whispered, "I'll have you! You fucking twat."

There was no more trouble. Wicket and Fly had their breakfast and ate until they both felt they could explode. It had to last them the rest of the day and in Wicket's case a couple of days more until his benefit was paid.

For the first time in a very long time Wicket felt happy. He looked at Fly and smiled. She smiled back and her eyes lit up.

"You're so beautiful," he said.

They stayed in the Day Centre until it closed at 1pm sharp. Then back out into the cold. Dog wagged his tail frantically and jumped up and down, so pleased he was to see them. Wicket bent down and gave Dog a couple of sausages which he'd squirreled away for him. He had some more in his coat pocket. Dog wouldn't go hungry.

The people in the town were battening down their shutters as talk of 'the beast from the east' was bandied about. There were amber weather warnings out as a bitterly cold front moved over the country from Siberia. That night they were forecasting temperatures of -8.

"We'll be ok," Wicket said, pulling Fly snugly towards him as they walked through the town heading for the cliffs, Dog running before them.

They were gazing into each other's faces so didn't immediately see Jack and two of his mates step out of a doorway and into their path.

Jack was holding a long iron. One of the others had a knife. Fly screamed.

Wicket pushed her. "Run!" he shouted.

Fly did. Running as fast as she could down the street.

Wicket had his own weapon. He hadn't been in Afghanistan for nothing. He pulled a Stanley knife out of his pocket and flicked the blade up. But he was too late. Jack's mate was behind him, pinning his arms against his back as the Stanley knife clattered to the ground.

Dog was snarling. He leapt at Jack who had taken a step towards Wicket.

"Fuck you!" Jack screamed and threw Dog aside. "Get him!"

The short thick set man with the knife grabbed Dog and, making sure Wicket had a good view, pulled Dog's head roughly back and cut his throat.

Wicket's "No!" reverberated off the walls of the houses and all down the street. He loved Dog. Dog had been his only reason for staying alive.

He gave a great roar as Jack began laying into him with the iron bar. The short man carelessly tossed the lifeless body of Dog aside. He laughed in Wicket's face and raised the knife still red with Dog's blood and carved a deep cut down Wicket's right hand cheek. Wicket slumped to the ground, blood all over him.

Some hours later Wicket regained consciousness. He was in a narrow alley way off the main street. It had just started snowing. He managed to pull himself onto the street just as a young couple laughing together were racing through the snow. The girl saw Wicket and screamed. There was a long trail of blood in the snow back to the alley.

The girl's boyfriend calmed her down and called an ambulance. Wicket didn't remember much else, just a vague sense of being picked up and put somewhere warm.

Wicket had concussion from his injuries and drifted in and out of consciousness for two days. The knife wound on his cheek had gone down to the bone and he had to have twelve stitches.

During the times he was conscious he worried about Fly. Where was she? Had Jack got her too?

As he was worrying a locum doctor came over to his bed and asked him how he was feeling.

"OK, good," Wicket said. "Go out now."

The young doctor shook his head. "Oh I don't think so. Let's keep you in another day or so. I'm still concerned about the blow to your head and you certainly don't want to be sleeping out in this weather."

Wicket looked over to the window. He could see heavy snow falling. All he could think about was Fly. Where was she?

Painfully he got out of bed. "Discharging myself," he said.

The doctor shook his head. "You're crazy!"

It was difficult walking. His head throbbed with every step. It was still snowing and the ground beneath was frozen hard and very slippery. Wicket kept slipping and ended up having to haul himself along the walls of the terraced houses. He was making for the Day Centre. He prayed that Fly was there.

Simon was on the door when Wicket staggered up.

"Christ!" he said. "You've had a good kicking."

Wicket didn't reply to that. "Fly?" he whispered. "Fly, is she here?"

Simon shook his head. "Not seen her, mate, not since Boxing Day. Didn't come here last night. We were open for rough sleepers."

Wicket's head shattered and fragmented like it had in Afghanistan.

He had an awful thought.

It took Wicket several hours to climb back up to the tent. The snow was like a blizzard and he kept falling on the slippery frozen grass. The temperature had dipped lower than it had reached for ten years touching -10 and -15 in the wind chill.

Wicket had no gloves. His hands were on fire but he didn't care. He couldn't get the awful thought out of his mind.

Finally he reached the tent. The front flap was zipped up. It took him several minutes to unzip it as his hands wouldn't work. At last he did it and he lifted the flap.

She was sitting up with the red blanket around her. Her face was turned towards him but she did not see him. Her eyes were frozen closed and her cheeks were frozen hard as marble. Fly's heart had failed her. She looked like a snow queen, an ice maiden.

Wicket's heart was failing too and his mind gave out.

He put his arms around Fly and pulled her as much towards him as he could. She was very stiff.

"It's OK my darling," he whispered. "I'll warm you up. You'll be fine."

He couldn't let her go. Not Fly, not when he'd just found her. He kissed her ice-cold lips. His own stuck to them. He kissed her frozen cheek and began to rock her as well as he could. He was humming to her, just some senseless tune over and over. Humming and trying to warm her up.

A lone dog walker found them days later like that, frozen together. Her dog had barked at the tent and she lifted the front flap and screamed. Icicles in their hair, icicles coming from their eyes.

The Day Centre organised a small memorial ceremony weeks later on the top of the cliffs. They thought it was a nice idea to scatter the ashes of Wicket and Fly over the edge into the sea beneath.

Whoever could manage the steep climb came from the Day Centre to mourn two of their own. Dragging sleeping bags and black bags, nearly forty homeless people made the climb to pay their respects, all except Jack. He'd disappeared from the area that night.

And every year on the anniversary of Wicket and Fly's death as the light of dawn falls on the Day Centre, there on the cold stone steps lie two red roses which someone has laid there in the night.

The End

Women Of The Spring

~~~~~

Great Pan is in mourning. Over the length of the centuries he has aged. Once, when the shadow of the cross lay over the earth, the world wept and cried, 'Great Pan is dead!' But on the third day he returned to bite at the Spring. His teeth were perfect then, small even corals. On the third day his eyes upturned were moonstones flecked. But now, alone in the sad, brown forest which chokes as it breathes, he is silent, motionless, mourning.

The stench of his breath is terrible. His teeth are crumbing away. The tips of his ears once jaunty, are savaged and the dense green fronds of his hair wither, their roots shot with decay. Down his cheek falls an emerald tear and another. And soon, near his black, clipped hooves half eaten, caught in one last shaft of brilliant sunlight, his tears form a pool of stagnant green. And Great Pan squats on his haunches and scoops at the water which flashes in sun-sparks, which glitters through the thin green spines of his fingers. And he bends and drinks insatiable from the pool of his own bright tears.

Then the Great Pan rises strong in the growing wind, for he believes he has heard Spring moving, gathering her great green skirts to scatter the sweet bud of life. Then his head falls and a tear falls as he listens and it is not Spring jostling that he hears but his own mother weeping, deep in the earth. Weeping as she heaves up the new shoots to the curve of the world, green shoots, yellow-tipped with decay. His mother is dying: she is rotting away.

Pan remembers the birth of the world. From a still dark distance he had watched as his mother laboured in pain. As she opened her proud dark thighs, rich with fecundity and, in a rush of blood, the world spilled out. "O my son," she had said. "You must nurture the Spring. She is yours to cleave to your soul." But now Spring is ailing, now she is crippled, her soul blackened and rank with decay. And his mother is dying, putrifying, deep in the gut of the world, rotting away.

By the emerald pool of his tears a woman lies naked, moist and open to take the Great God Pan, to turn the axis, to re-start the engine. Pan lifts his head and there deep in the secrets of his eyes, men are writhing and screaming: women distraught, writhing, weeping, impaled on the throes of birth. But the birth is still-born, the baby deformed, mutilated, rank and decayed.

By the emerald pool of Pan's tears the woman lies naked and beckons the dead. And through the pool of his tears Pan goes to the woman, to thrust his rank seed into the woman and then, with a whimper of pain, to turn away. Then his head falls and a tear falls as he listens to his mother weeping for the green shoots yellow-tipped with decay: listens to her dying, deep in the axis of the earth, rotting away. Soon now all his children will be still-born: soon now all his children will be mutilated. And one day, as the years gather up, like a flaccid grey fungus Pan will be impotent.

But deep in the gut of the world his mother is wild in her death throes. Pan is resigned but she will never resign herself. Not she who thrust the world in blood and pain through darkness. And now she turns and the curve of the world rips apart. And through that great chasm she screams her anguish to the women of the world. And on the curve of the world that great scream rushes like a tempest and uproots those same trees that the mother had heaved to the surface.

So tired now in her wild death throes but a warrior still. She takes a drink and the great oceans drain into the gut of the world where the mother lies dying, lies rotting away.

And on the curve of the world the great fires of the sun rage through the forest. And in the forest Pan watches and waits, charged now with the grandeur of gladness. His bloodied hooves trip at the chasm of the curve and down he hurtles, down to the dear wild arms of his mother, dying.

On the curve of the world the woman stands gazing down the centuries, down the gathering of the years, naked, motionless.

And the dying mother heaves open her eye-lids and the curve of the world grinds and quakes. Up through the chasm the mother reaches, up through the centuries, through the gathering of the years, up to the woman.

Again Pan watches from a dark still distance as the mother, in a voice both hoarse and bloody, speaks before she dies, before she falls back into the darkness onto Pan whom she extinguishes.

"I have fought and I have fought. Tell them I'm dying. I bequeath you the gift of the Spring. Cleave her to your bosom; nurture her in your heart; cup her gently this broken bird in the warm nest of your bright dawn. It is your legacy. Speak it to the world. Hurry! A last call to arms..."

The End

Dancing A Dark Dance

There'd been a murder in the house which made it very difficult to sell. It had been on the market for two years. Fay hadn't been back once. She wasn't allowed to initially because it was all sealed up by forensics. Then she didn't want to because even the thought of the house threatened to bring it all back. She couldn't bear it. It had to stay locked up with chains and padlocks in her mind.

That Friday the estate agent called her and said she might really need to think about auctioning the land. The house was getting beyond repair and it had such a bad name locally. What he didn't say was that he'd had a nasty experience there the previous day.

"It might help," he continued, breathing heavily into the phone," if they'd be able to convict someone. That might have put a lot of things to rest."

Fay smiled a slightly twisted smile. The Estate Agent was still talking but she wasn't really listening. Despite her best intentions she'd started thinking about the house. And about Tom and, of course, about Mother dearest. She might have to take a last look to congratulate herself on doing the right thing.

She remembered the day she met Tom. Mother had invited him round to give her an estimate for replacement windows in the big house. Fay had opened the front door. He was really quite good looking. Tall with a dark complexion and a bit of a lob-sided face.

He gave Fay such a lovely warm smile and right down to the tips of her toes she tingled. She was twenty-five but she'd never had a boyfriend. In fact she hadn't many friends at all. Mother, glamorous Mother, had always called her a funny little thing. Some people thought she might be autistic. Her mother felt she really wasn't someone to be proud of having as a daughter. While her mother still enjoyed life and had boyfriends, Fay stayed at home when she wasn't working. She never met anyone in her job cataloguing artefacts at the museum so when Tom appeared at her front door with his aura of masculinity and raw energy, she was done for.

Mother came up behind her.

"For goodness sake, Fay, ask the poor man in."

Fay stepped aside. Her mother was dressed up to the nines, hardly appropriate for a meeting with a double glazing salesman But there you are; that's how she was.

She was in her fifties but you could have mistaken her for an early forty year old. Her skin was beautifully smooth still and her hair only slightly helped by some golden streaks. She wore it loose and long and she could get away with it. Everyone was always saying how wonderful she was. Fay stared at her as Tom came into the hall. She felt so dull next to her with her own mousey locks and the puppy fat around her middle which had never gone away.

Tom smiled at her again. She couldn't understand it.

After a while Mother soon lost interest in Tom when the estimate was almost double what she'd expected. She waved Tom away and it was left to Fay to see him out.

He paused on the door-step and turned to Fay. "I knew I'd seen you somewhere before. It's just come to me. You work in the museum!"

Fay was so surprised she laughed out loud. "Goodness. I didn't think I was visible."

"You shouldn't put yourself down," Tom said quite gently and flashed her another of his sun-kissed smiles.

And that's how it started. He asked her out for coffee and over the next few months their friendship blossomed into a relationship. Mother made fun of her remorselessly. She couldn't understand why any man would be interested in her daughter, particularly when she was around.

Now, back in Mother's wild garden, the warm June air was tumbling about, frisking through the thickets of soft greenery but it would not penetrate the crumbling white house. It wouldn't gambol passed the fluted porch columns which were tottering and veering westwards towards the sinking sun.

She remembered Tom standing there the first time he kissed her. He'd had his back to the sun which gave him a glowing halo all around his head. She remembered the feel of his firm lips on hers. She remembered her shock of delight as he slid his warm tongue right into her mouth.

Now, once inside the house Fay felt a shiver of cold marble, of dampness, of darkness mingled with a strange sensation almost like suppressed excitement; an excitement flown off somewhere, almost trapped in the crumbing bricks. Voices, echoes, almost. She shivered. Everything was coming back.

She went through to the old kitchen, remembering how once it might have been so dear to her. Mother dearest making tea and toast, tending the chicken broth which was simmering on the old stove. But then she remembered what it tasted like that chicken broth. She could feel the bile rising in her throat. She hated it. Sometimes she'd thought her Mother was trying to poison her. She could never believe Mother cooked at all. It was so out of character.

A flash of a memory came back to Fay. Her mother at the stove turning round to smile at her as she lifted the horrible broth off the cooker and placed it on the table in front of Fay. Fay remembers how she would always smile back at her mother so she would never suspect what was going on inside her. Little had she known of the plans Fay would make about her mother every night to soothe herself to sleep. This is how they'd lived, just the two of them, dancing a dark dance.

Now there was a scurry of little clawed feet as Fay ducked under the splintering beams and the curtains of cobwebs. Nothing to see of the mice and rats, of the spiders and snails and centipedes, all busily making their nests now in what had purported to be Fay's home.

In the hall Fay paused, remembering so well tying school laces, all left thumbs. Remembering lots of comings and goings, red satin dresses for birthday parties, reluctant returns from school. But mostly she remembered Tom standing there in the hall and Mother dearest sat waiting at the bottom of the stairs. Fay shook herself. Don't think that! All was well. All had been lovely.

Now in the hall there were bluebirds flying about high in the rafters. They'd brought the sun to peep in up there through the oriole window, through the gaps in the roof where the blue tiles had been. Bluebirds singing, trapped bright and high in the shaft of dusty sunlight.

The drawing-room's stout door lurched from one hinge. The door that had shut Fay away from any talk and gaiety which very occasionally might have gone on in there. The infant in Fay was pleased that the door hung so disconsolately. But then she remembered once laughter coming from the drawing-room. She remembered pressing her ear against the cold wood, trying to hear what Mother was saying. She remembered when it suddenly went quiet and then the door was flung open with such violence that she nearly fell into the room.

Mother had glared down at her. Behind her, on the sofa, Fay had seen a man.

"Get to your room!" Mother had said. "I'll deal with you later."

Fay winced now, stood there in the dust and the cobwebs, remembering just how her mother dealt with her. But then something turned again in her mind and locked away the thought as so many thoughts had been locked away over the years.

She shook her head and remembered how wonderful Mother had been, how perfect. The most perfect Mother in the world. And a tragedy what happened to her.

As she squeezed through the doorway around the lurching door, the first thing she noticed in the drawing-room was a coat draped over the chair-back, over the white cast iron conservatory chair which was in the middle of the drawing room. Nothing else in the long room, only echoes of the past, louder here. Fay shivered and looked around her. She could almost reach out and pluck the voice from the dusty air: she could almost catch the echoes in the crumbling bricks, the bricks that held the secret.

It was a woman's coat. A black great-coat similar to her Mother's old one on the white chair and something was resting on top of the coat. It was like art, Fay thought. Suddenly everything crystalised into inevitability.

On the top of the coat was a large spray of Chinese jasmine. Its fragrance filled the room. Suddenly Fay felt she was breathing jasmine through her skin, drinking it in. A large spray with small white flowers like stars of the East, the leaves shining green and rustly.

Memories flooded back. Fay's childhood had been filled with the fragrance of jasmine, an ironic juxtaposition to everything else. All through the long summers it would come to Fay, sliding in past the white net curtains billowing in the breeze in her room up in the loft. It would come to her in her afternoon naps and would sometimes wake her in time for tea so she didn't get into trouble. Up from the old conservatory it climbed all over the walls until the old conservatory blew down; until they dumped all the old white cast iron chairs and table; until they hacked at the roots of the jasmine, dragging it out of the ground.

And now, again, it's back. And the chair's back. And where did the coat come from? Such a large spray of jasmine, such fragrance dancing again over the floorboards, once varnished, once golden, now splintering. And the fragrance of jasmine almost personified, spinning and weaving round the drawing-room, a hurricane to the senses, making Fay's mind reel about. Making her almost remember what for two years had been locked away.

And the black coat... Its collar was velvet. It wasn't old. It was not rotting away like the house. Yet it belonged here.

The sun was sepia through the dusty bay windows: it was not a June sun in here. It was a faded sun of death and dying. It was heavy and spoke of over-ripe apples rotting sweet in the long hot grass. The tired sun settled on the empty fireplace, on the dusty old grate as if it remembered the heat of the past before Fay and her mother's time; the crackle of logs, the blue plume of apple-wood smoking, the burnt crumpets, the wet muddy dogs steaming asleep. Even the old mantel-piece is crumbling away, its carvings splitting into jig-saws, its proud inlays turning into sawdust. The in-laid panels of stained glass are cracked and broken, their leaded trims missing, their colours dim and hopeless.

Something was happening to Fay's head. Something was worming its way to the surface of her consciousness.

She remembers now. It had been a Thursday. She'd come back early from work with a migraine. She'd called out to Mother but no answer. She'd thought she heard voices from upstairs and laughter.

She had gone upstairs slowly, her head throbbing and her vision distorted by the migraine.

On the top step she paused. The door to Mother's room was slightly open. She could see a naked pair of legs. And buttocks, muscular male buttocks, thrusting. She couldn't see the head or the face but she didn't need to. They were the only male buttocks she had ever seen in her life and they belonged to Tom. And Tom was naked in Mother's room thrusting, thrusting into Mother.

Fay must have screamed as she pushed the bedroom door wide. It came just as Tom and Mother reached the pinnacle of their pleasure and were crying out. But as they cried out Tom turned his head and saw with horror Fay standing there.

He leapt off Mother who was lying naked in the crumpled sheets. She stared at Fay.

"Get out of my room! What the hell are you doing here?"

She was less non-plussed than Tom. He had some moral decorum and at least looked quite ashamed as he tried to struggle into his jeans.

He took a step towards Fay.

"Don't touch me!" she screamed. "Get the fuck out of here!"

Mother laughed. She had never heard Fay swear.

Fay's fists were bunched up hard as she glared at her naked mother.

So full of hate and rage she was and so intent on what she was about to do that she barely noticed Tom slip passed her. She didn't hear the front door close behind him. She didn't hear him running down the path. Nor did she hear the squeal of brakes as the white BMW rammed straight into Tom as he ran out of the gate.

Now, as Fay stood there in the middle of the drawing-room, that's when it came. A clear sound like a church bell calling to Fay from the hall. Calling her name. "Fay, Fay." Mother's voice.

Fay gasped. She told herself off for the power of her imagination but she thought she'd just have a quick look in the hall to be on the safe side.

The blue birds were still singing in the rafters but there was something else. A faint hint or imprint of a face high up there. A shimmering shadow of a face, caught for an instant but then was gone.

Fay frowned. She would not be frightened by her or intimidated by her ever again. Never again. She was proud of herself. They couldn't prove it but the case was closed. It was assumed Tom had done it and that he was running away when the BMW hit him. He'd had Mother's DNA on him and she had his DNA and his semen on her. But everyone said he'd seemed such a nice man and going out with the daughter too. How could he have done something as unspeakably violent as that?

Fay had got away with it.

She went back into the drawing-room. Such a buzzing of memories now flying out of the crumbling bricks; flying around the flaps of brocade wallpaper still stuck, here and there, to the walls. A torrent of memories which Fay could not still. And everywhere, always, the fragrance of jasmine, penetrating, trapped in the bricks, locked up in the walls.

Fay couldn't bear it. She covered her ears with her hands but not before she saw the coat had gone. The white cast-iron chair was still in the middle of the room but there was nothing on it. Around it the large spray of jasmine had been brutally torn apart. It lay in shreds and fragments on the floor beneath the chair, but of the coat there was no sign.

She rushed into the garden where the June sun gambolled about. The garden was waiting and when Fay turned to look at the house she knew why.

It was impossible, a trick of light, an hallucination. But whether it was a hallucination or not what Fay saw was Mother, large as life, stood in the doorway smiling that impossible hateful smile.

"Come darling," she said. And behind her was a shadow, a figure bigger than her mother. The shadow of Tom.

Fay froze in fear but even so she felt an irresistible pulling and a tugging coming from somewhere. And before she knew it she was back in the house. And the black coat was back in the drawing-room in the rush of memories gambolling about.

She remembered everything now of that afternoon two years ago. She remembered it all, the betrayal and its aftermath in gory technicolour. And as she remembered she heard a roar starting in the basement. Like a huge animal waking from a long sleep the old house heaved itself up. The very walls started falling, collapsing inwards. The ceilings fell in with a huge rumbling crash. Everything was crumbling and settling into rubble and Fay was buried beneath. The air was thick with dust. Nothing much was visible. It was impossible to distinguish what made that movement in the corner of the drawing-room beyond the piles of bricks and coloured glass.

But as the dust settled it was possible to see amidst the splintered wood and clumps of bricks, amid the broken grate and the dirt and the dust, the chair: the white cast-iron conservatory chair standing upright and proud. And on the chair the black coat had come back and on the coat the jasmine was back as a wonderful spray, its fragrance rising and drifting over the rubble.

As it drifted a soft chattering voice could be plucked from the ruins together with a dim sound like Mother's laughter.

But then the fragrance of jasmine was dissolving, was lifting and drifting away. The voice stilled and with a last faint laugh Mother dearest split into a million specks of dust.

The End

A Moving Story

Ideally Marion would have taken Henry with her to view the property, particularly the garden. Gardens were important to Henry.

The Estate Agent was waiting for her by the white gate

"So sorry," Marion said. "The traffic was awful." Marion spent her life apologising and hated herself for it. Every time someone banged into her in a supermarket or trod on the back of her heel she said 'sorry' and could kick herself.

She would like to stand in the cereal aisle and roar. She would like to take a machine gun and mow down all the shoppers. She'd like to tell them all to fuck off.

But of course she never did any of those things. They weren't nice.

The estate agent was young with a long blonde plait hanging down her back. She smiled at Marion. "I think we've met before. Last year?"

It was all a blur to Marion. She vaguely remembered she'd been moving then but it had all fallen through at the last minute. She hadn't been that bothered. It was excruciatingly painful thinking of leaving the house with its memories of Samantha. She'd vowed that was the end of it. She would stay put. But here she was again starting out on the process. Part of her was opting for life. She kept telling herself. It would do her good. To get away from that house and all the awful memories. All that time ago before she met Henry.

She remembered the Estate Agent then. Marion had insisted on a lift from one property to another. The Estate Agent hadn't wanted to as she wasn't in a company car so wasn't insured. She resisted for a couple of minutes but despite Marion being a person who apologises all the time, another part of her being can be very forceful. Quite bullying in fact. She knew it was because of her low self esteem and sense of powerlessness but it didn't come over like that and was the main reason for the failure of a number of intimate relationships in her life. Apart from her marriage to Robin, but the tragedy had ended that. But, so what, she often thought about the ones before. None of them were worthy of her and she had Henry now so everything was perfect.

"Let's go in. I'm Janice by the way, " the Estate Agent introduced herself and handed Marion the property details.

Half an hour later they were still there, Marion full of ooohs and ahhhs. She absolutely loved it. She was supposed to be down-sizing but in fact this was up-sizing. An extended bungalow with three bedrooms, one ensuite. Bliss! And so much space. She was absolutely sure Henry would love it. And the garden was divine. A long lawn with mature trees and flowerbeds. And a greenhouse; and a shed; and a wooden summerhouse.

Marion could see Henry and herself sat out there with a glass of Sauvignon Blanc on a warm summer evening. As the brochure said the summerhouse was west facing, just right to catch the last glimpses of the sun as it threaded the sky with reds and golds and pinks and sank to sleep beneath the sea.

"We'd better go," Janice said. "I've got another viewing."

"Sorry," Marion said, of course. "I love this house. I really want it. I wish I could make an offer today but I suppose I need to find a buyer for mine first."

She couldn't wait to get home to tell Henry all about it. And to show him the pictures of the beautiful garden.

He was sleeping when she arrived home. She didn't like to wake him as it was very warm so she got on to her Estate Agent instead and dropped the price of her own house. Marion can be a very determined woman when she wants. Robin her ex had always said that and he was right. She'd gone through three lots of IVF before she fell pregnant. They were both over the moon when it worked and nine months later she gave birth to a lovely little girl who they named Samantha.

"She looks like you," Robin had said. Marion was cuddling Samantha at the time and she felt that life could never get more perfect.

Samantha was three when it happened. Robin was taking her to the park while Marion cooked the Sunday lunch. The car which hit them was going very fast. The driver was breathalysed after and found to be over the limit from his drinking the night before. He was sentenced to three years at the trial. Three years for killing a little girl of three.

Samantha didn't die immediately. She lay in a coma for some weeks, her little body hooked up to various machines connected to her nose, her heart and other parts of her. Marion would never forget the hiss, bomp of the breathing machine.

Robin didn't die though Marion would probably have preferred that to losing Samantha. He suffered a couple of broken ribs and a fractured collarbone. The hospital only kept him in overnight. After that both Robin and Marion spent most of their days sat by Samantha's bed, praying.

The day the doctors turned the machines off was a Tuesday. That always seemed so strange to Marion. Tuesdays seemed such ordinary, mundane days not fitting for something so profound and momentous as the death of her dear little girl.

The days between Samantha's passing and the funeral were a complete and utter blank to Marion. Robin was left to make the funeral arrangements. Marion had nothing in her. All she could remember of the funeral afterwards was the tiny coffin in which they buried Samantha. Burial was the one thing Marion insisted on. She could not bear the thought of burning her lovely little girl's body. She'd been so careful with Samantha around anything hot in case she hurt herself. Better she thought for Samantha to go to sleep in the ground where she would become a part of nature. Marion tried for days to remember a poem she'd learnt at college. She googled various words and finally found it. It was by Wordsworth and included the lines 'Rolled round in earth's diurnal course With rocks and stones and trees.' That was the best thought she could hold in mind of Samantha held within earth's diurnal course. It also meant there was a grave for Marion to tend and sit beside through the long months and years following Samantha's death.

Robin tried to reach Marion. Devastated himself, he nevertheless tried to comfort her. He would try and hold her, stroke her hair, make her nice meals. He even suggested taking her on holiday to the Caribbean. She heard none of it, responded to none of it. If he touched her she flinched and shivered and pushed him away. She blamed him even though she knew rationally it wasn't his fault. But like an endless refrain in her mind the words kept coming: if you hadn't taken her to the park that Sunday; if you hadn't taken her to the park that Sunday; if you hadn't taken her to the park that Sunday.

One Thursday they had a huge row. Robin couldn't bear his life. He'd lost his little girl and he'd lost his wife. He knew she blamed him. He blamed himself even though he knew it wasn't his fault.

"I hate you!" Marion screamed at him. "It's all your fault!"

He tried to kill himself that night with an overdose of paracetemol and whiskey. He didn't do it at home, being a considerate type of person, surprising for a bailiff. He didn't want Marion to find him.

He felt it was a cliché but nevertheless he drove to the car park near Beachy Head and settled down to stop living. He'd managed to swallow about fifty paracetamol and drink nearly half the bottle of whiskey when a land-rover pulled into the car park and doused its lights. Robin could vaguely hear through the fog of pills and alcohol, some laughter. He glanced blearily out of the window at the man and woman climbing out of the land-rover. The man was undoing his zip and the woman lent against the driver's door and lifted her dress. Just as the man was going to enter her she saw Robin watching. She whispered something to the man who zipped himself up and strode angrily towards Robin's car. They were so intent on their desire that they hadn't even noticed Robin parked there.

Robin was sectioned and detained in hospital for six months. Initially in any moments of lucidity he hoped Marion would visit him. She never did. They divorced a year later.

Very occasionally Marion would think about Robin and wonder where he was. But with any thought of him, the pain of losing Samantha which suffused her heart worsened until she thought the pain would cause a heart attack. Not that she would have minded that much. She had little to live for.

Three weeks later Marion received an offer on her house. She was over the moon although it wasn't quite what she'd hoped. However she had learnt things from Robin the bailiff and negotiated a deal with Janice the Estate Agent who was selling the bungalow.

It was at times like this that Marion wished she had some women friends to share the moment. She used to have friends but she given them all up after Samantha passed.

She prepared a special meal for Henry and described the house and the garden again for the zillionth time. Henry looked interested but it was difficult for him to do anything other than eat when his favourite meal was in front of him.

The months passed and one buyer fell out of the chain. Marion was distraught and thought the whole enterprise would collapse. Luckily another buyer came along very quickly and the process all kicked in again.

On the day of completion Marion could not stop weeping. She knew she needed to leave her house, the house Samantha had lived in but it was so hard. She kept telling herself that she wasn't leaving Samantha behind. Samantha was profoundly and intricately knitted into the fabric of Marion's being. She breathed Samantha. She felt her own last word to leave her lips when it was time for her own passing, would be 'Samantha'.

She closed her front door for the last time, locked it and walked away.

The removal men were ace. Two of them were musicians and did removals to supplement their incomes. They made Marion laugh which was no mean feat. She did feel excited. The house was everything she'd hoped for, as perfect as it could ever be without a little blonde girl running up and down the stairs.

They'd unloaded everything by 4pm. Marion shut her new front door and turned to Henry.

"Isn't it fantastic?" she said.

Henry looked up at her with his green eyes. "Miaow," he said.

The End